The Big Honey Hunt

by Stanley and Janice Berenstain

COLLINS

Trademark of Random House, Inc., William Collins Sons & Co. Ltd., Authorised User

12 13 14 15 16

ISBN 0 00 171326 4 (paperback)
ISBN 0 00 171125 3 (hardback)

© 1962 by Stanley and Janice Berenstain
A Beginner Book published by arrangement with
Random House, Inc., New York, New York
First published by Great Britain 1966

Printed & bound in Hong Kong

We ate our honey.

We ate a lot.

Now we have no honey

In our honey pot.

Go and get some honey.

Go and get some more.

Go and get some honey

From the honey store.

We will go for honey.
Come on, Small Bear!
We will go for honey
And I know where.

The store . . .
She said to
Get it there!

Not at the store.
Oh, no, Small Bear.

If a bear is smart,
If a bear knows how,
He goes on a honey hunt.
Watch me now!

How do you hunt it?

How, Dad, how?

If a bear knows how,

If a bear is smart,

He looks for a bee

Right at the start.

Bees hide their honey

In trees that are hollow.

So we will find

A bee to follow.

9

Is that a bee?

He went, "Buzz! Buzz!"

BZ-Z-Z

He looks like a bee.

Why, yes!

He does.

B-Z-Z-Z

We will follow that bee . . .

We will follow that bee . . .

12

We will follow that bee
To his honey tree.

That tree!

Is that a honey tree?

It looks like one
So I know it's one.
Sit down, Small Bear,
And watch the fun.
Small Bear, you watch
Your smart old Dad
Take out more honey
Than you ever had.

Are you getting honey?
Are you getting a lot?
Will we take home honey
In our honey pot?

That is not
A honey bee!
That was not
A honey tree.

B-z-z-z

B-z-z-z

The bee!

The bee!

There goes the bee!

19

On with the honey hunt!
Follow your Pop.
Your Pop will find honey
At the very next stop.

B-Z-Z-Z

We will follow, and follow . . .

And follow along!

I will find a new tree
And I won't be wrong.

Is that a honey tree?

How do you know?

Well, it looks just so.

And it feels just so.

Looks so. Feels so.

So it's SO!

Now watch, Small Bear.

I am about

To take that

Good old honey out.

How are you doing?

Are you getting a lot?

Are you getting much honey?

Or are you not?

BZ-Z-Z

Wrong kind of tree!
Wrong kind of tree!

Look, Dad!
There goes
Your friend the bee!

29

On with the hunt!

I will not rest.

I will follow that bee

To his honey nest!

When a bear is smart,

When a bear is clever,

He never gives up.

And I won't, ever!

Dad!

Is that

A bee tree there?

33

I know it is.

Why, yes, Small Bear.

It can't be wrong

Like the last tree was.

Only a bee tree

Goes, "Buzz! Buzz!"

Are you getting honey?
Are you doing well?
Or is something wrong?
I smell a smell.

36

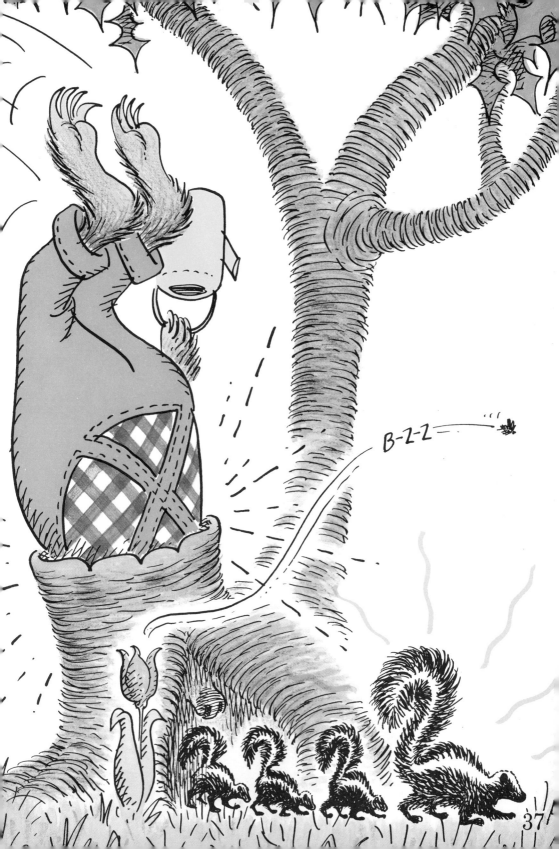

B-Z-Z

The bee!

The bee!

I see the bee!

B-Z-Z-Z-Z

If you want to get honey,
There is just one way.
You must follow your bee
If it takes all day.

If a bear is smart,
If a bear is bright,
A bear keeps going
If it takes all night.

B-Z-Z-Z

He went in there!
Your friend the bee!
He went in there!
Is this our tree?

Now let me think.

Now let me see . . .

This looks just like

A honey tree.

And . . .
    It feels
    Just like
    A honey tree.

And . . .

It goes, "Buzz! Buzz!"

Like a honey tree.

B-Z-Z

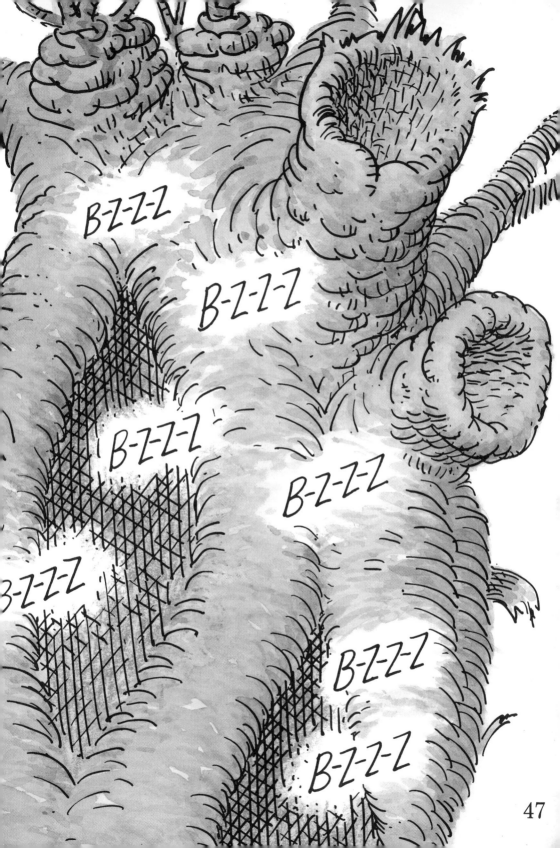

B-Z-Z-Z

B-Z-Z-Z

-Z

-Z-Z-Z

And . . .

It tastes

Just like

A honey tree!

And so

You see

This tree must be—

Must, must, must be

A honey tree!

49

I never saw
More honey! Never!
Now don't you think
Your Dad is clever?

I think you are
Very clever, Dad.
But your friends the bees
Are very mad!

But Dad!

You left

The honey there!

It was not
The kind I want,
Small Bear.

I will get you honey.

I said I would.

But that bee's honey

Was not too good.

Where are you going
To find the honey?
Here in the water?
Now that seems funny.

No, we won't find honey

In here, Small Bear.

But soon, very soon

I will show you where.

When the bees have gone,

We will go along, too.

Your Dad is smart,

And he knows what to do.

But how will you
Do it, Dad?
How, Dad? How?

The best sort of honey
Never comes from bees.
It comes from a store.
I would like some,
Please.